Cleveland

CAVALIERS

BY JIM GIGLIOTTI

The Child's World®
childsworld.com

Published by The Child's World®
1980 Lookout Drive • Mankato, MN 56003-1705
800-599-READ • www.childsworld.com

Cover: © Joe Robbins.
Interior Photographs ©: AP Images: Eric Risberg 5; Tony DeJak 6, 12,
18, 21; Walter Green 9; John Amis 10; Phil Long 26. Dreamstime.com:
Den Krut 13. Imagn/USA Today Sports: David Richard 26, Ken Blaze 26,
Derick Hingle 26. Newscom: Phil Masturzo/TNS 17, 29; Curtis Compton/
MCT 22.

ISBN 9781503824515
LCCN 2018964196

Printed in the United States of America
PA02416

ABOUT THE AUTHOR

Jim Gigliotti has worked for the University
of Southern California's athletic department,
the Los Angeles Dodgers, and the National
Football League. He is now an author who
has written more than 100 books, mostly
for young readers, on a variety of topics.

TABLE OF CONTENTS

GO, CAVALIERS!

The Cleveland Cavaliers were on top of the NBA just a short time ago. In 2016, they were league champions. They gave Cleveland its first pro sports title in 52 years. They had LeBron James. He was the game's top superstar. James left the team after the 2018 season. Now the Cavs are trying to find their way back. Who will be the team's next big star?

LeBron James holds up his NBA Finals MVP trophy while clutching the 2016 NBA championship hardware.

Larry Nance Jr. drives to the basket against a Central Division rival, the Indiana Pacers.

WHO ARE THE CAVALIERS?

The Cavaliers play in the NBA Central Division. That division is part of the Eastern Conference. The other teams in the Central Division are the Chicago Bulls, the Detroit Pistons, the Indiana Pacers, and the Milwaukee Bucks. The Cavs won the division four years in a row starting in 2015. They have finished in first place seven times in all.

WHERE THEY CAME FROM

The NBA has 30 teams now. However, it had only 14 in the 1970 season. The league added three **expansion teams** the next year. The Cavaliers were one. A Cleveland newspaper had a fan poll to name the team. The fans chose Cavaliers. A cavalier is a soldier on horseback. The team name is often shortened to Cavs. The Cavs made the **playoffs** for the first time in 1976.

9

The Cavaliers battled the Celtics during the 1976 Eastern Conference playoffs.

Matthew Dellavedova pushes the Cavaliers past the Atlanta Hawks in an Eastern Conference showdown.

The Cavaliers play 82 games each season. They play 41 at home and 41 on the road. They play four games against each of the other Central Division teams. They play 36 games against other Eastern Conference teams. They play each of the teams in the Western Conference twice. Each June, the winners of the Western and Eastern Conferences play each other in the NBA Finals.

WHERE THEY PLAY

The Cavs play at the Quicken Loans Arena. It was built where a huge marketplace used to be. It is next door to Progressive Field. That is where baseball's Cleveland Indians play. The team has two **mascots**. One is named Moondog. The other is named Sir C.C. Moondog got its name from a rock-and-roll DJ. The Rock and Roll Hall of Fame is in Cleveland.

800.820.CAVS • CAVS.COM

The **Q** **Quicken** **Loans** Arena

The Cavs' home is nicknamed "The Q." Inside, fans get help cheering from the team's mascot, Moondog.

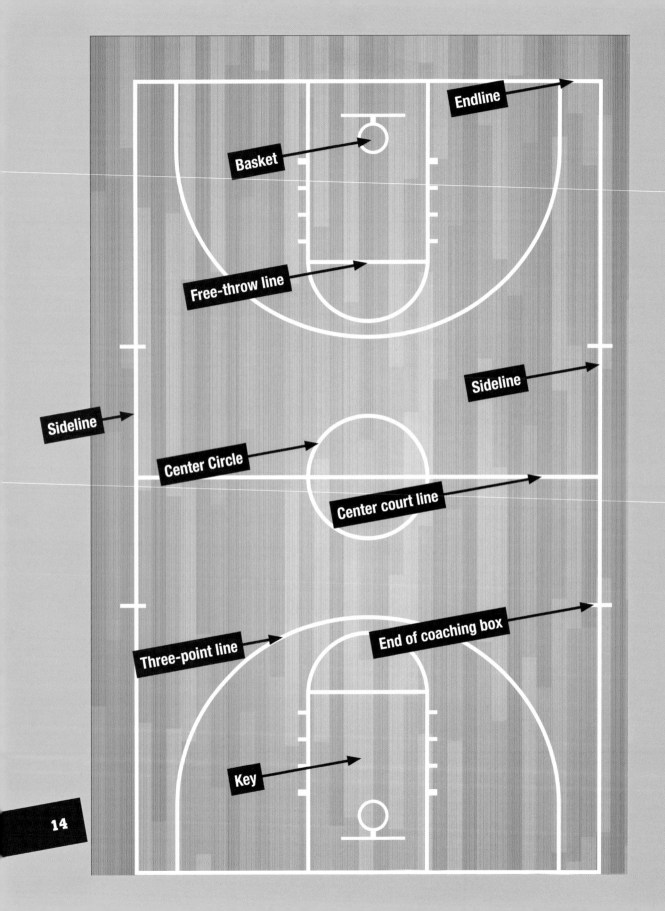

THE BASKETBALL COURT

An NBA court is 94 feet long and 50 feet wide (28.6 m by 15.24 m). Nearly all the courts are made from hard maple wood. Rubber mats under the wood help make the floor springy. Each team paints the court with its **logo** and colors. Lines on the court show the players where to take shots. The diagram on the left shows the important parts of the NBA court.

How big is "The Q" in Cleveland? It would take more than 53 million basketballs to fill it!

GOOD TIMES

The Cavs had many firsts in 1976. They had their first winning year. They won a playoff series for the first time, too. In 2016, the team won its first and only NBA title. Kyrie Irving made the winning shot in the last game. In a 2017 game against Portland, Kevin Love scored 34 points. That was just in the first quarter! He finished with 40 points. The Cavaliers won 137–125.

Kyrie Irving's great shooting touch helped the Cavaliers beat the Golden State Warriors for the 2016 NBA title.

After LeBron James turned his back on Cleveland in 2010 and 2018, the team struggled to win games.

TOUGH TIMES

Michael Jordan made a shot at the **buzzer** against the Cavs in the 1989 playoffs. That gave the Bulls a series win. It was a tough loss for the Cavs. At least that team was in the playoffs. The Cavs missed the playoffs seven years in a row starting in 1999. The 2003 team won only 17 games. But the toughest times came when LeBron James left the Cavs to play for other teams.

ALL THE RIGHT MOVES

LeBron James' top move was blocking shots from behind. He made a huge block in Game 7 of the 2016 Finals. James also was one of the best ever at the cross-court pass. He could spot an open teammate on the other side of the court. Current big man Kevin Love also is a great passer. Sometimes his passes go all the way from one end of the floor to the other.

In basketball, a "big man" means a player who is tall and strong. It can also refer to a team's best player.

Kevin Love launches a perfect chest pass. The big man's skill at passing helped the Cavs win.

Before each game, LeBron James tossed hand-drying powder in the air.

HEROES THEN

When fans think of the Cavaliers, they think of LeBron James. "King James" is one of the best players ever. The Cavaliers have had other great players, too. Mark Price is second to James in team history for three-pointers, **assists**, and steals. Brad Daugherty was a five-time all-star center. Kyrie Irving was a big-time scorer.

Veteran Kevin Love became the team's main player in 2019. He can rebound and play defense inside. He can also shoot and score from the outside. The Cavs drafted Collin Sexton in the first round in 2018. He runs the offense at **point guard**. Tristan Thompson protects the rim at **center**. He is a big rebounder.

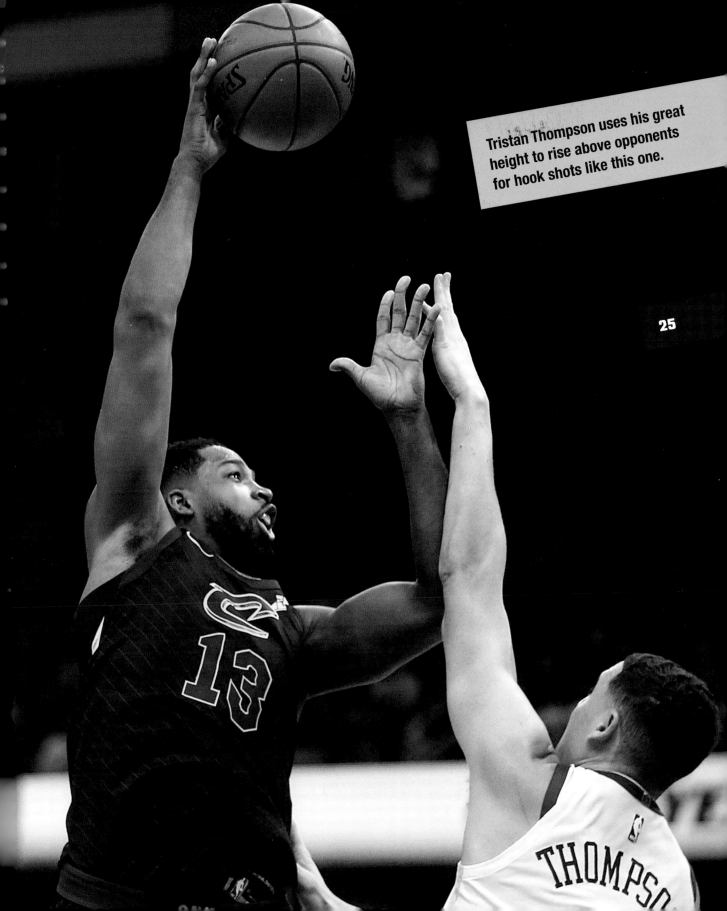

Tristan Thompson uses his great height to rise above opponents for hook shots like this one.

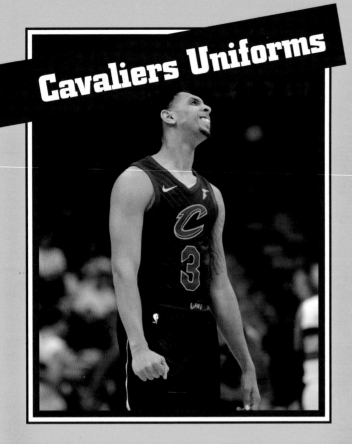

WHAT THEY WEAR

NBA players wear a **tank top** jersey. Players wear team shorts. Each player can choose his own sneakers. Some players also wear knee pads or wrist guards.

Each NBA team has more than one jersey style. The pictures at left show some of the Cavaliers' jerseys.

The NBA basketball is 29.5 inches (75 cm) around. It is covered with leather. The leather has small bumps called pebbles.

The pebbles on a basketball help players grip it.

H ere are some of the all-time career records for the Cleveland Cavaliers. These stats are complete through all of the 2018–19 NBA regular season.

GAMES	
LeBron James	849
Zydrunas Ilgauskas	771

POINTS PER GAME	
LeBron James	27.2
World B. Free	23.0

ASSISTS PER GAME	
Andre Miller	8.2
Lenny Wilkens	7.7

REBOUNDS PER GAME	
Rick Roberson	12.0
Cliff Robinson	10.5

STEALS PER GAME	
Ron Harper	2.3
Brevin Knight	2.0

FREE-THROW PCT.	
Mark Price	.906
Mo Williams	.891

THREE-POINT FIELD GOALS

LeBron James	1,251
Mark Price	802

LEBRON JAMES

GLOSSARY

assists *(uh-SISTS)* passes that lead directly to a basket

buzzer *(BUZZ-er)* a loud signal that goes off at the end of a quarter, half, or game

center *(SEN-ter)* a basketball position that plays near the basket

expansion teams *(ex-PAN-shun TEEMS)* in sports, teams that are added to an existing league

logo *(LOW-go)* a team or company's symbol

mascots *(MASS-kots)* costumed characters who help fans cheer

playoffs *(PLAY-offs)* games played between top teams to determine who moves ahead

point guard *(POYNT GARD)* a basketball player who most often dribbles and passes the ball

tank top *(TANK TOP)* a style of shirt that has straps over the shoulders and no sleeves

veteran *(VEH-ta-rin)* a player with several years of experience

FIND OUT MORE

IN THE LIBRARY

Doeden, Matt. *The NBA Playoffs: In Pursuit of Basketball Glory.* Minneapolis, MN: Millbrook Press, 2019.

Fishman, Jon. *Basketball Superstar: LeBron James.* Minneapolis, MN: Lerner Books, 2018.

Goodman, Michael E. *Cleveland Cavaliers (NBA Champions).* Mankato, MN: Creative Paperbacks, 2018.

ON THE WEB

Visit website for links about the Cleveland Cavaliers:
childsworld.com/links

Note to Parents, Teachers, and Librarians: We routinely verify our Web links to make sure they are safe and active sites. So encourage your readers to check them out!